MAY 21 2009

BILLINGS CO SCHOOLS LIBRARY

3 3121 00126 2356

P9-DTB-782

743.89623
Sautter, Aaron.
How to draw crazy fighter
planes

WITHDRAWN
DICKINSON AREA PUBLIC LIBRARY

EDGE BOOKS™

DRAWING COOL STUFF

HOW TO DRAW

CRAZY FIGHTER PLANES

by Aaron Sautter

illustrated by Rod Whigham

BILLINGS COUNTY PUBLIC SCHOOL
Box 307
Medora, North Dakota 58645

Capstone

Mankato, Minnesota

Edge Books are published by Capstone Press,
151 Good Counsel Drive, P.O. Box 669, Mankato, Minnesota 56002.
www.capstonepress.com

Copyright © 2008 by Capstone Press, a Capstone Publishers company.
All rights reserved. No part of this publication may be reproduced in whole
or in part, or stored in a retrieval system, or transmitted in any form or by any
means, electronic, mechanical, photocopying, recording, or otherwise, without
written permission of the publisher.
For information regarding permission, write to Capstone Press,
151 Good Counsel Drive, P.O. Box 669, Dept. R, Mankato, Minnesota 56002.
Printed in the United States of America

Library of Congress Cataloging-in-Publication Data
Sautter, Aaron.
    How to draw crazy fighter planes / by Aaron Sautter; illustrated by Rod Whigham.
    p. cm. — (Edge books. Drawing cool stuff)
    Includes bibliographical references and index.
    Summary: "Lively text and fun illustrations describe how to draw crazy fighter
planes" — Provided by publisher.
    ISBN–13: 978-1-4296-1298-2 (hardcover)
    ISBN–10: 1-4296-1298-3 (hardcover)
    1. Airplanes, Military, in art — Juvenile literature. 2. Drawing — Technique —
Juvenile literature. I. Whigham, Rod, 1954– II. Title. III. Series.
NC825.A4S28 2008
743'.896237464 — dc22   2007025103

Credits
Jason Knudson, set designer; Patrick D. Dentinger, book designer

1 2 3 4 5 6 13 12 11 10 09 08

TABLE OF CONTENTS

WELCOME!

You probably picked this book because you love fierce fighter planes. Or you picked it because you like to draw. Whatever the reason, get ready to dive into the world of crazy fighter planes!

Ever since World War I (1914–1918), airplanes have been used to fight battles in the sky. The first warplanes were simple, single-engine planes with cheap machine guns that jammed a lot. But today's fighters are deadly, high-tech machines. They are packed with powerful guns and missiles to quickly dominate the skies over a battlefield.

This book is just a starting point. Once you've learned how to draw the different planes in this book, you can start drawing your own. Let your imagination run wild, and see what sorts of fearsome fighter planes you can create!

To get started, you'll need some supplies:

1. First you'll need drawing paper. Any type of blank, unlined paper will do.

2. Pencils are the easiest to use for your drawing projects. Make sure you have plenty of them.

3. You have to keep your pencils sharp to make clean lines. Keep a pencil sharpener close by. You'll use it a lot.

4. As you practice drawing, you'll need a good eraser. Pencil erasers wear out very fast. Get a rubber or kneaded eraser. You'll be glad you did.

5. When your drawing is finished, you can trace over it with a black ink pen or thin felt-tip marker. The dark lines will really make your work stand out.

6. If you decide to color your drawings, colored pencils and markers usually work best. You can also use colored pencils to shade your drawings and make them more lifelike.

P-51 MUSTANG

Of all World War II (1939-1945) warplanes, perhaps the most important was the P-51 Mustang. It was fast, maneuverable, and easy to build. More than 15,800 P-51s were built for the war. The Mustang gave the United States and England a strong advantage.

After drawing this plane, try giving it a special paint design of your own!

STEP 1

STEP 2

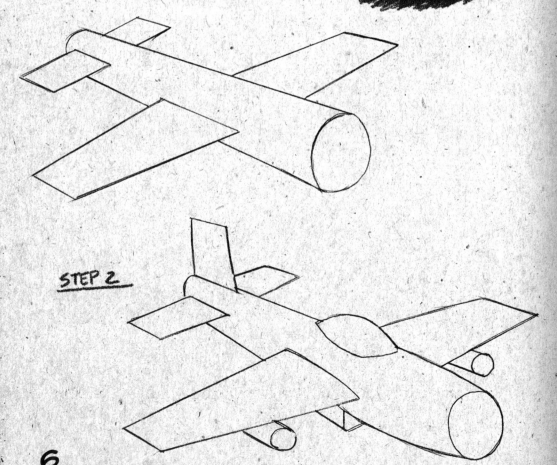

6

STEP 3

STEP 4

FINAL!

P-38 LIGHTNING

The P-38 Lightning was one of the most useful U.S. fighters in World War II. It was used mainly for long-range missions over the Pacific Ocean. Its twin-engine design made it very stable, so pilots could target the enemy more accurately.

When you've mastered this plane, try drawing it again in fierce combat!

STEP 1

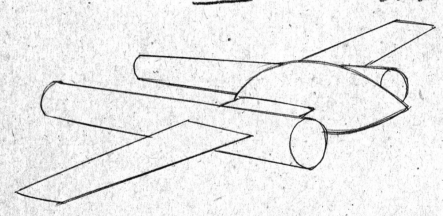

STEP 2

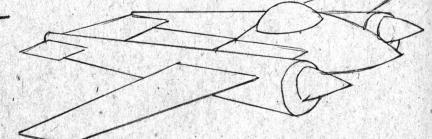

STEP 3

STEP 4

FINAL!

9

P-80 SHOOTING STAR

The P-80 Shooting Star was the United States' first jet-powered fighter plane. Its first combat action was in the Korean War (1950–1953). It reached speeds of 600 miles per hour and carried heavy machine guns and missiles.

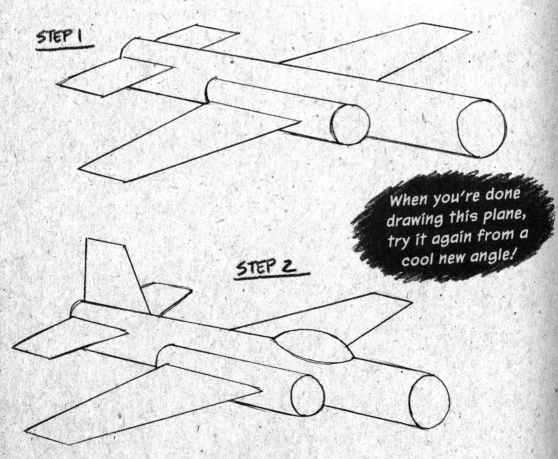

STEP 1

STEP 2

When you're done drawing this plane, try it again from a cool new angle!

STEP 3

STEP 4

FINAL!

11

RUSSIAN MiG-15

The Soviet Union created the MiG-15 in the 1950s. It was one of the fastest and deadliest warplanes of its time. It flew faster than 650 miles per hour and was armed with machine guns and rockets.

After drawing this plane, try showing it doing some cool moves in the air!

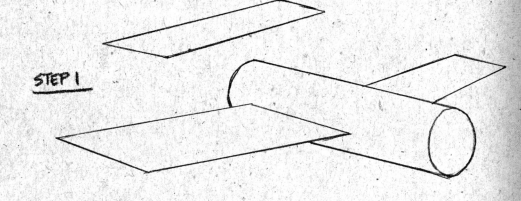

STEP 1

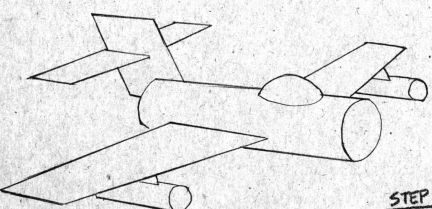

STEP 2

STEP 3

STEP 4

FINAL!

13

SR-71 BLACKBIRD

The SR-71 Blackbird was a sleek and stealthy spy plane built in the 1960s. It was one of the fastest and highest-flying airplanes ever made. It could fly up to 85,000 feet high at more than 2,200 miles per hour!

After drawing this plane, try making your own top-secret spy plane!

STEP 1

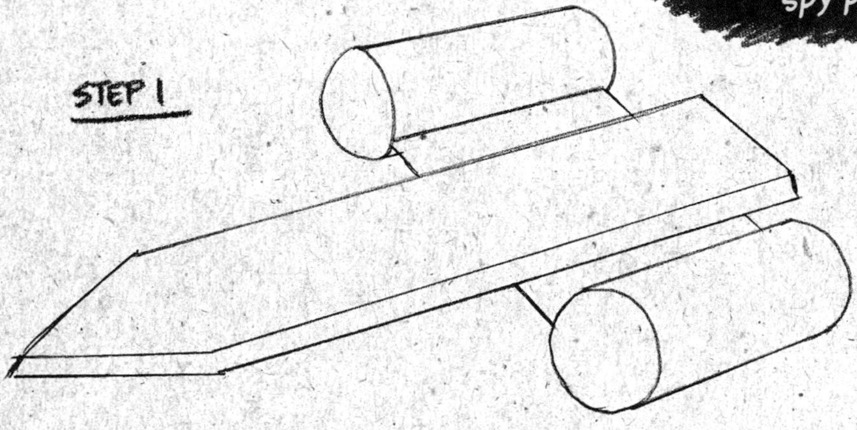

STEP 2

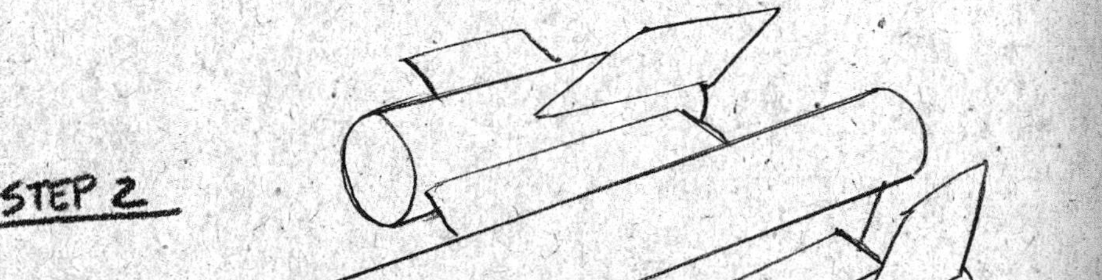

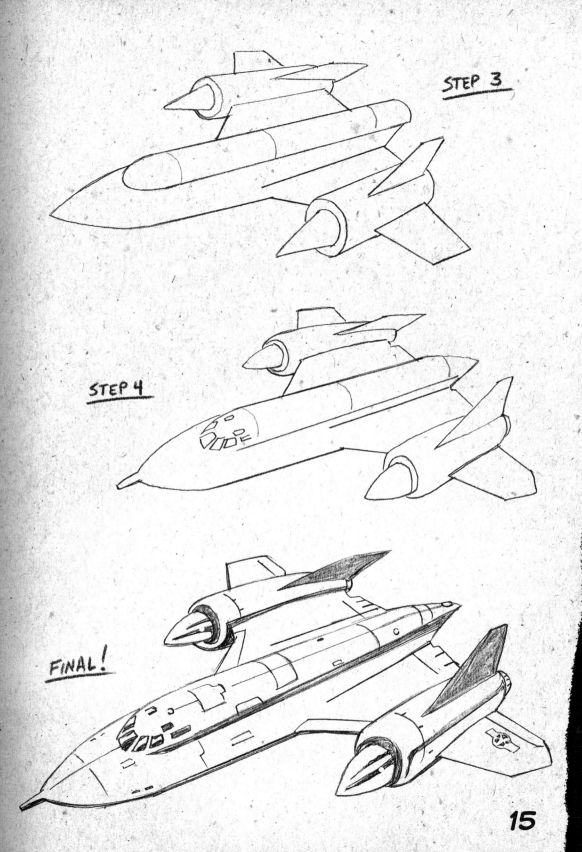

STEP 3

STEP 4

FINAL!

15

B-2 SPIRIT

Look! Is that a UFO? No, it's the futuristic B-2 Spirit. This stealthy bomber is designed to avoid detection by enemy radar. And it can fly up to 6,000 miles without refueling.

After practicing this plane, try it again flying over a secret enemy base!

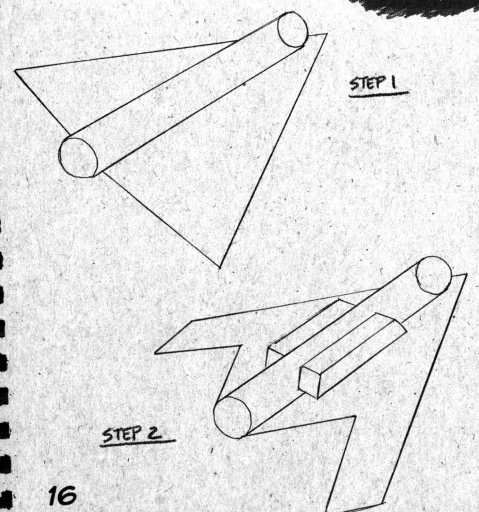

STEP 1

STEP 2

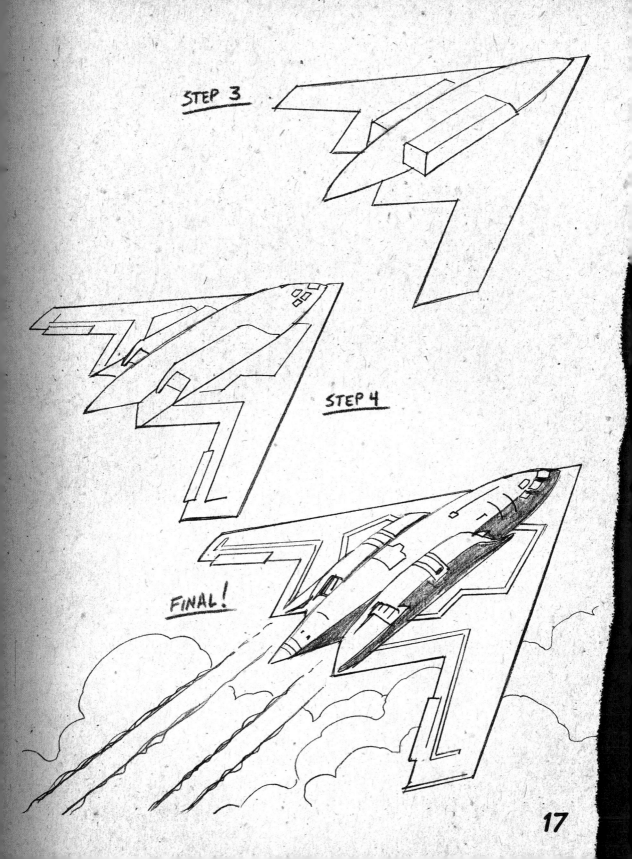

STEP 3

STEP 4

FINAL!

17

F-4 Phantom II

The F-4 Phantom II was the main U.S. fighter plane during the later years of the Vietnam War (1954-1975). Its sleek body and powerful engines helped it set several speed records. One Phantom even flew at twice the speed of sound!

After practicing this plane, try giving its nose a cool new paint design!

STEP 1

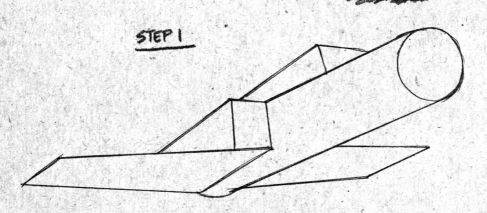

STEP 2

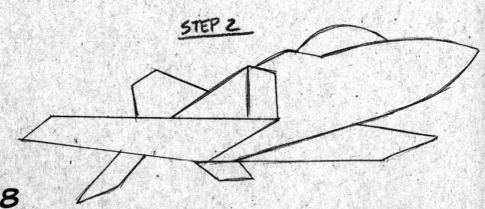

STEP 3

STEP 4

FINAL!

AV-8B HARRIER

The AV-8B Harrier jump jet is unique. It's the only U.S. jet fighter that can take off and land vertically. It doesn't need a runway, so it's often used where other aircraft can't go. It carries a large variety of missiles and bombs.

After drawing this plane, try it again landing at your local park!

STEP 1

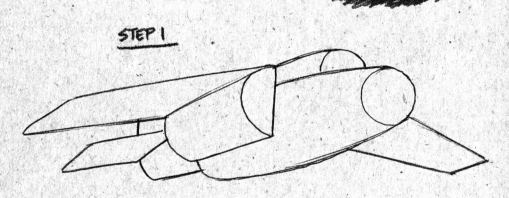

STEP 2

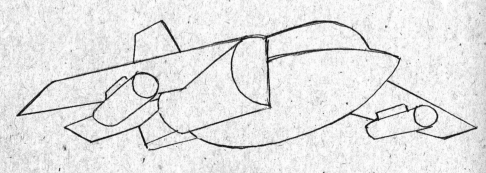

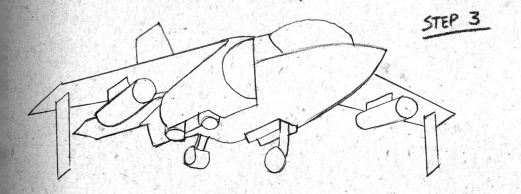

STEP 3

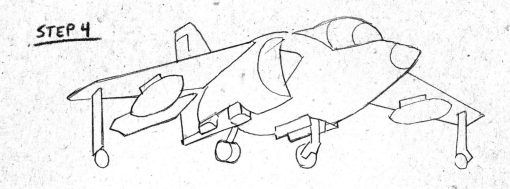

STEP 4

FINAL!

A-10 "WARTHOG"

The A-10 Thunderbolt is often given the nickname "Warthog" because of its fierce appearance. This fighter is more like a flying tank than an airplane. It carries a large variety of weapons. And its forward machine gun can shoot up to 4,200 armor-piercing rounds per minute!

After you've mastered this plane, try it again in action over a battlefield!

STEP 1

STEP 2

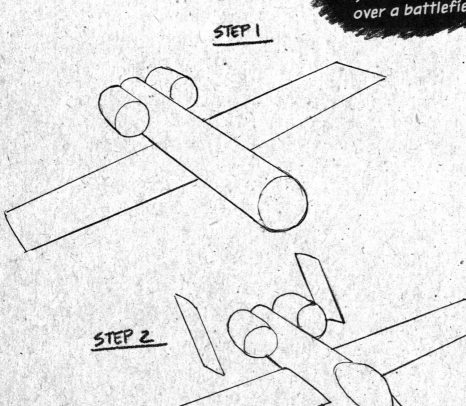

STEP 3

STEP 4

FINAL!

23

K-17 Hornet

In the future, warplanes will be even more amazing than today's fighter planes. The K-17 Hornet's radar jammers will let it fly safely over the enemy. And its powerful lasers will easily destroy tanks and other war machines.

When you're done drawing this plane, try it again fighting in a big battle!

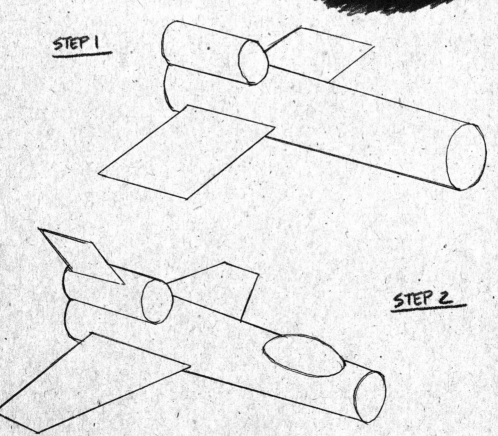

STEP 1

STEP 2

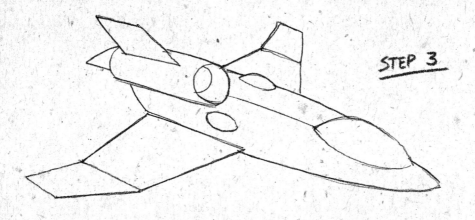

STEP 3

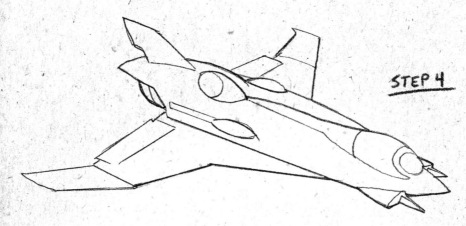

STEP 4

BILLINGS COUNTY PUBLIC SCHOOL
Box 307
Medora, North Dakota 58645

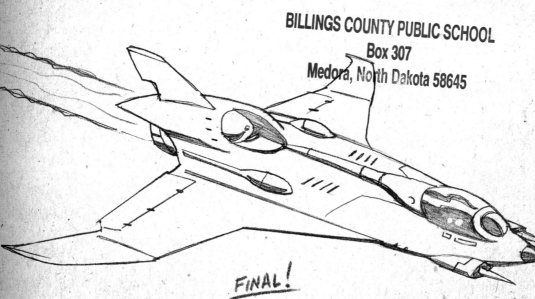

FINAL!

25

DOGFIGHT!

The "Red Baron" was one of Germany's deadliest pilots during World War I. Many French and British pilots feared getting into a dogfight against his famous red triple-winged plane. The Baron was so skilled that he had at least 80 victories in air combat! But the Baron's luck ran out. He was killed in action on April 21, 1918.

When you're finished drawing this dogfight, try it again with some of the other planes in this book!

STEP 1

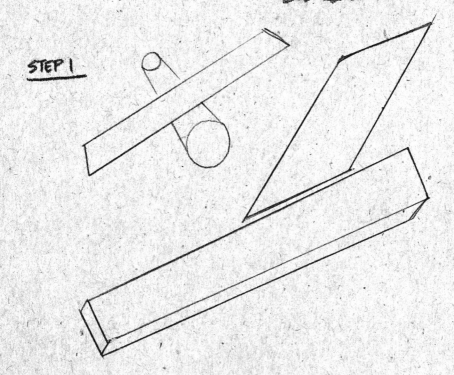

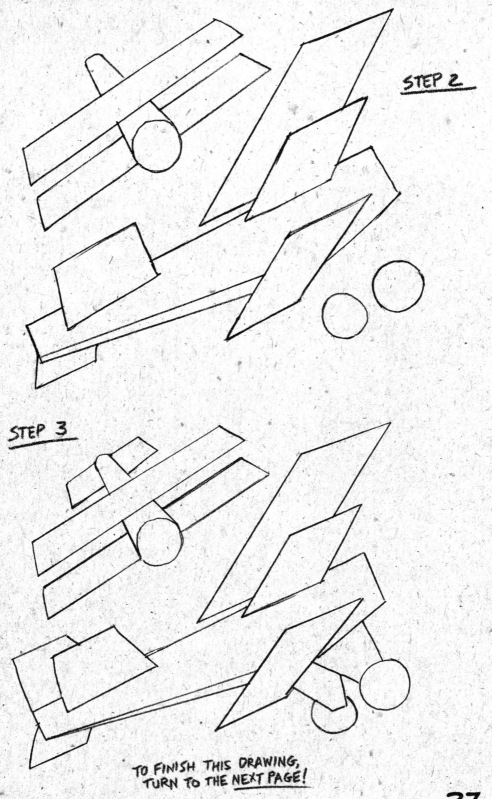

STEP 3

TO FINISH THIS DRAWING,
TURN TO THE NEXT PAGE!

STEP 4

STEP 5

28

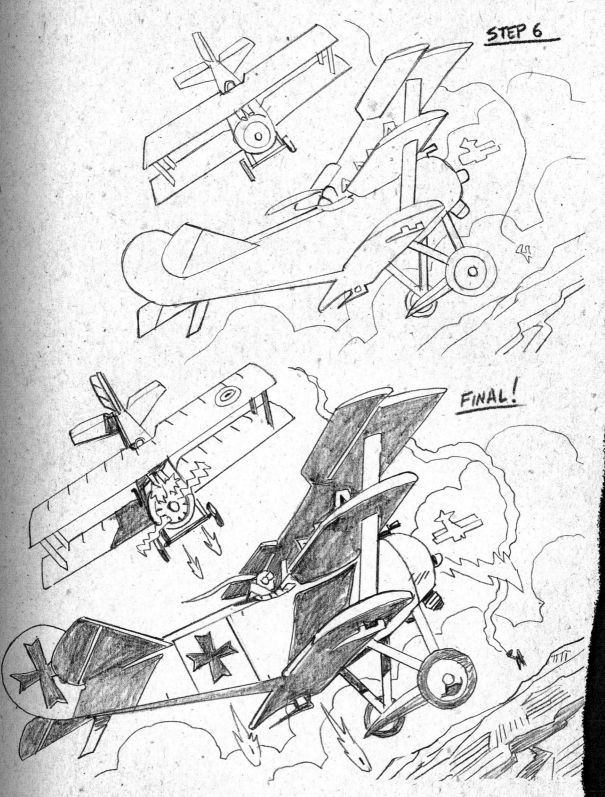

STEP 6

FINAL!

29

GLOSSARY

dogfight (DAWG-fite) — a mid-air battle between fighter planes

laser (LAY-zur) — a powerful, high-energy beam of light

maneuverable (muh-NOO-ver-uh-buhl) — able to move easily

missile (MISS-uhl) — a flying weapon that blows up when it hits a target, such as an enemy plane

mission (MISH-uhn) — a planned military task

radar (RAY-dar) — equipment that uses radio waves to find distant objects

stealthy (STEL-thee) — to move secretly and quietly

UFO (YOO EF OH) — an object in the sky thought to be a spaceship from another planet; UFO is short for Unidentified Flying Object.

unique (yoo-NEEK) — one of a kind

READ MORE

Barr, Steve. *1-2-3 Draw Cartoon Aircraft: A Step-by-Step Guide*. 1-2-3 Draw. Columbus, N.C.: Peel Productions, 2005.

Court, Rob. *How to Draw Aircraft.* Doodle Books. Chanhassen, Minn.: Child's World, 2007.

Walsh, Patricia. *Aircraft*. Draw It! Chicago: Heinemann, 2006.

INTERNET SITES

FactHound offers a safe, fun way to find Internet sites related to this book. All of the sites on FactHound have been researched by our staff.

Here's how:
1. Visit *www.facthound.com*
2. Choose your grade level.
3. Type in this book ID **1429612983** for age-appropriate sites. You may also browse subjects by clicking on letters, or by clicking on pictures and words.
4. Click on the **Fetch It** button.

FactHound will fetch the best sites for you!

INDEX